Edward Hopper's GREAT FIND

Story and Pictures by JOAN ELIZABETH GOODMAN

For Keith,
My love and inspiration.

A GOLDEN BOOK • NEW YORK
Western Publishing Company, Inc., Racine, Wisconsin 53404

Edward Hopper collected all the odds and ends and little lost things that most Meadowtown folks didn't even notice.

He had buttons and bottle caps, pebbles and Popsicle sticks, string, stamps, safety pins, and rubber bands. Anything that was handsome or interesting or useful became part of The Edward Hopper Collection.

One morning Lucy Softpaws came to Edward's collection with the blouse she had just finished making.

"Edward, you have such nice furry ears," she said. "And you have so many buttons. Could I please have some itty-bitty plain white buttons for my blouse?"

Even though his ears turned pink, Edward said, "No. I don't like to break up my collection."

"My blouse won't look nearly as sweet without your buttons," said Lucy. "Besides, you have so *many* buttons. Pretty please!"

"Well," said Edward, "just this once."

"Thank you oodles!" purred Lucy. Off she went with three of Edward's favorite pearl buttons.

On another day Hillary Squeak pounded on Edward's door.
She shrieked, "HELP! HELP! I've run out of fishhooks!"

"Oh, Hillary," said Edward, "you're always in a pickle! You
know this isn't a lending collection."

"Yes, I know," said Hillary. "But I can't go fishing without
fishhooks."

"All right," said Edward. "You can use some of my safety pins. But remember, bring them back!"

"You betcha!" said Hillary. But she never brought back the safety pins.

When it was too rainy for basketball, Frankie Pudwoggle had lunch at the collection. Edward showed him his newest, most beautiful stamps.

"These are classy!" said Frankie. "But I'd rather be at dribbling practice."

"WATCH OUT!" shouted Edward. "You *are* dribbling. You're dribbling jelly on my stamps!"

"A little jelly won't hurt them," said Frankie.

It did. Edward got so mad his ears turned bright red.

"I've had enough!" he said. "Lucy takes my best buttons, Hillary never returns my safety pins, and you drip jelly on my stamps. From now on, no one comes near my collection."

The next day Edward posted signs all over Meadowtown. They said,

THE EDWARD HOPPER COLLECTION
IS CLOSED!
NO BEGGING, NO BORROWING.
KEEP OUT!!!

Edward pulled down his shades, locked his door, and that was that. No one came to bother The Edward Hopper Collection anymore.

Edward went collecting every day. He searched all over Meadowtown, from Low Meadow through Ravenswood and back to the Piney Grove Picnic Grounds.

"My collection gets bigger and better every day," said Edward one afternoon. "But something is missing. I need a really great find for my collection."

Edward got up early the next morning and went to the junkyard behind Hillary's cabin. He inspected all the broken carts and wrecked wagons. He sifted through barrels and boxes. All he found were three paper clips, a chipped marble, and a bent teaspoon.

"This stuff is boring," said Edward. "I need something
spectacular for my collection." So Edward kept on searching.

He climbed over and under and around piles of junk.
Edward searched until he was dirty and tired and ready to
give up. Just then he spotted something shiny poking out from
under a worn tire.

"Eureka!" shouted Edward. He pulled out the biggest safety pin he had ever seen. "This is what I've been looking for! And wouldn't Hillary love it!"

Edward imagined Hillary trying to use the giant safety pin as a fishhook. He laughed all the way home.

He put his new pin in the box with all the others.

"It certainly is big," he said. "But it doesn't seem special enough. My collection needs something else."

"Maybe if I sort it all out," he thought, "I will discover what is missing."

Edward began with his buttons. He emptied the button jars onto his desk. He carefully sorted the buttons according to shape and color. Edward had many fascinating buttons, and among them was the first treasure he had ever found.

"My rose!" he said, picking up an exquisite pink button shaped like a tiny rose. "This was Lucy's favorite. It made her purr like crazy." Edward gently put the rose away. He put all the buttons away. He didn't feel like sorting anymore.

"It's nice knowing what I have," he said with a sigh. "But I still don't know what I'm missing. Maybe tomorrow I'll find what it is."

Edward woke up feeling hopeful. He was on his way out when he noticed a letter in his mailbox. It was from his cousin Hedda.

"Nothing important," said Edward. Then he saw the stamp. "WOW! A basketball stamp! Just wait till I show Frankie."

Then he remembered. The Edward Hopper Collection was closed. Frankie would never see the stamp. Lucy wouldn't see the rose button. Hillary wouldn't see the giant safety pin. No one would see any of the new or old treasures.

"I miss sharing my collection. I miss my friends. If only they could be more careful." Edward sat on the porch and puzzled it out.

GRAND Reoper.
ToDAY!!!
The New And Improved
Edward Hopper
...llection.
...ne,
...Com..., All!

"That's it! If they can't be careful, I can!" Edward raced inside and got to work on his plan. Pretty soon there were new signs all over Meadowtown. They said,

GRAND REOPENING
TODAY!!!
THE NEW AND IMPROVED
EDWARD HOPPER COLLECTION.
COME ONE, COME ALL!

Edward raised his shades, threw open his door, and waited.
Before long all of Meadowtown came to celebrate the grand
reopening. Lucy brought a cake. Frankie brought his
basketball. And Hillary brought back all the safety pins she
had ever borrowed. Edward was so happy his nose twitched.

"Greetings, Meadowtown!" began Edward. "The New and Improved Edward Hopper Collection will be in two parts—the museum for viewing, and the lending collection for trading and borrowing."

"Hurray for Edward and the new museum," purred Lucy.

"Hurray for the lending collection," cheered Hillary.

"Hurray!" shouted Frankie. "A basketball stamp!"

"Welcome back," said Edward. "The collection is better
when you're here to share it. And now let the party begin!"